The Reward of Childhood Truth

~and the story of~

Little Mary's
First and Last Falsehood

Grace & Truth Books

Sand Springs, Oklahoma

ISBN # 1-58339-060-x
Originally published in the 19th Century
Current edition, Grace & Truth Books, 2004

All rights reserved, with the exception of brief quotations.
For consent to reproduce these materials, please contact the
publisher.

Cover art by Caffy Whitney
Cover design and layout by Ben Gundersen

Grace & Truth Books
3406 Summit Boulevard
Sand Springs, Oklahoma   74063
Phone: 918 245 1500

www.graceandtruthbooks.com
email: info@graceandtruthbooks.com

Table of Contents

"No proof, Mr. Benson! No Proof!
Why, isn't a stick a proof?"

Truth Insures The Future For Charles And Harry

Chapter 1

TRUTH ON TRIAL

"Boys will be boys," said Mr. Arnold.

"Very true, Sir," answered Mr. Benson. "At least they are not likely to be girls nor women. This doesn't mean, however, that boys must necessarily be thieves and liars."

"I have said nothing about thieving and lying," said Mr. Arnold in haste.

"Nor mischievous?" asked Mr. Benson.

"Oh, I don't know, Mr. Benson. Boys are naturally mischievous," replied Mr. Arnold.

"Are they though?" asked Mr. Benson, dryly.

"Why of course they are" said Mr. Arnold. "Did you ever know a boy who wasn't as full of mischief as an egg is full of meat, as the old song goes?"

"I do not know how the old song goes, Mr. Arnold, but I have known boys who were not full of trouble. I have known boys who were noted for generosity, gentleness, kindness, and good manners," replied Mr. Benson.

"Meaning your own boys, I suppose," rejoined Mr. Arnold with a light laugh, not altogether a pleasant one.

"No, I am not speaking of my own boys, my good friend. I have lived long enough to know that parents are not always good judges of their own children's character."

"I am glad you admit that much, Sir," replied Mr. Arnold.

"And why shouldn't I admit that much? Parents may sometimes make mistakes and tend to be overly tolerant on one hand and to boast on the other. We are able, however, to speak facts."

"Just so, and I am here to speak about facts," said Mr. Arnold. "You cannot deny the fact that my *Prodigium Mundi* is broken down, killed, totally destroyed."

The speaker said this in a tone of anger which almost called up a smile on Mr. Benson's face. He restrained, however, and only said, "I do not deny the fact, Sir. I assure you that I am sorry for your loss, but I ask you to be just. You have no proof that my sons did the mischief."

"No proof, Mr. Benson! No proof! Why, isn't a stick a proof? Look at this, Sir!" Producing a big piece of wood from under his coat, he displayed it almost proudly. "I found this almost under the plant, Mr. Benson. It had cut the stem close to the root, and there it lay. I would rather it had fallen upon my head, I assure you."

"I cannot argue the fact of the stick, Mr. Arnold, but ..."

"Oh, I am glad you don't question that, Sir. I fancied perhaps you might," said the angry plant owner.

"The stick does not tell whose hand threw it. It could have come from somewhere else, couldn't it?"

"Well, Mr. Benson, I see how it is. You will take your boys' side, right or wrong. A great fool I was to come live next door to a parcel of boys."

"Really, Sir," said Mr. Benson rather warmly, "you are becoming very upset over a small matter. If I wanted to reply, I would say that no one asked you to come live next door to a parcel of boys. That would only, however, multiply words without wisdom. I admit you have some reason to feel annoyed."

Mr. Arnold agreed, "Yes, Sir, I have. My *Prodigium Mundi* ..."

"Was a very fine plant and would have been finer, no doubt ..." cut in Mr. Benson.

Mr. Arnold continued, "Not another like it in the country, Sir, for miles and miles around. I could have cried when I saw the ruin that it had come to. It was lucky for the lads that they were out of sight at the time, I assure you, Sir."

"You persist in saying that one of my sons did the damage then, Mr. Arnold?"

"I have not the least doubt of it, Sir. If I could prove it, I would! What's the use of saying what I would or wouldn't do? Of course, I can never prove

3

it. When boys set upon doing mischief, there's no bounds to their cunning. They made sure that nobody saw them," said Mr. Arnold.

"I beg your pardon, Sir. You are mistaken. It can easily be proved," replied Mr. Benson.

"Ah, indeed, and how?" asked the other gentleman.

"Simply by asking the boys a plain question when they come home from school, as I will do in your presence."

"What question, Mr. Benson?"

"I will merely ask if either one of them threw a stick into your garden last night," said Mr. Benson.

"You think you will get the truth from them in that way, do you, Sir?"

"I have no doubt of it, Mr. Arnold," returned the other, calmly and confidently.

"You will believe them if they say no, I suppose?"

"Most certainly, Sir," said the father.

Mr. Arnold laughed. It was a laugh as near to disbelief and scorn as politeness and good manners would allow. Perhaps it was rather too near to this. Mr. Benson was quick to notice it.

"I say again, Sir," he added. "I shall firmly believe what my sons tell me about this or any other subject. I have taught the boys to speak the truth, Mr. Arnold, and they do speak the truth."

"I don't doubt your thinking so, friend Benson, but boys will be boys, you know."

4

They were arguing in a circle. This obvious judgment of Mr. Arnold, which could mean anything or nothing, only brought the two men back to the point where they began. Mr. Benson saw this. He felt that Mr. Arnold was becoming needlessly angered, so he avoided any further argument. He said, "I shall ask my boys when they come home from school, Sir. Then you can hear what they have to say for themselves. For now, good morning." After this, Mr. Benson entered his own house. Mr. Arnold left his neighbor to return to his garden to mourn over the damage done to his *Prodigium Mundi.*

As you may have gathered, Mr. Arnold and Mr. Benson were next-door neighbors. They lived a few miles out of London, England in adjoining villas, or small houses. The two houses were attached to each other, but they were separate from any other neighboring houses. They had neat little flowerbeds in front and large gardens behind. The two houses were called "Park Villas."

Mr. Benson had lived in his Park Villa longer than Mr. Arnold, although he was younger in age. Mr. Benson was also by far the poorer of the two, He had lived five or six years at No. 1, Park Villas. When he first moved there, he was a sorrowing, heart-stricken widower. His wife had recently died leaving two very young sons to his care.

It is sad when a husband loses his wife and when children lose their mother. Since she had been very dearly loved it added to the grief for the

Bensons. In parting with her, her husband lost his kindest friend and wisest counselor on earth. The boys had to mourn the loss of a very tender parent and a caring guide and teacher.

Time, however, heals many sorrows. After some months had passed, the natural spirits of the boys recovered from the shock they had received. They loved the memory of their mother. They did not forget her instructions. They became, in part at least, adjusted to the loss of their mother. Of course, their father was thoughtful, warm, and giving. Over the years they almost stopped thinking of their loss, although the faint memory of their gentle mother did not erase from their minds.

Mr. Benson found it harder to accept the change in his life. In the highest and best sense, he had accepted his wife's death, for he was a Christian. He had learned to submit himself to God in humble faith that his Heavenly Father knew best. He had learned to say in his heart, "Father, not my will, but Thy will be done!" He had found it hard, however, to take over the new and heavy duties he had as a single parent. Very often, he found himself thinking very mournfully, though not rebelliously, "Oh if she had only lived! If she were only living now!" Yet, he trusted in the Lord. As often as this thought came into his mind, another thought followed it. "The Lord has done all things well," he whispered in his heart. He took comfort knowing that the wife he grieved for and missed so much was happy in heaven. So you see, although the widowed father sometimes felt sorrowful, he was always rejoicing as a Christian should.

I have said that Mr. Benson was a poorer man than Mr. Arnold; I mean poorer in worldly riches. Although Mr. Benson was educated and held a respectable position in life, he had to work hard for his living. With all his hard work, he could do no more than keep his small household in modest comfort. He wrote books as a profession. His books were popular as well as useful. Although they brought some profit to the people who sold them, the books did not make Mr. Benson rich by any means. This, however, is the way of the world. Mr. Benson did not complain.

The demand for Mr. Benson to work hard did not prevent him from paying attention to his two motherless boys. He and the boys went on long daily walks. Of course, their father had to leave them in the care of others for many hours each day while he worked. When they were very young, a God-fearing nanny watched over them. She also taught them to read and write. When they were about eight and nine years of age, Mr. Benson sent them to a school about a mile from home. They attended school from ten o'clock in the morning to four o'clock in the afternoon. Most evenings they spent with their father, but sometimes Mr. Benson had to work until late at night. On those nights the boys had to amuse themselves.

Charles and Harry Benson's father carefully taught his sons to speak the truth. Mr. Benson trained the boys to practice truthfulness for the health of their souls.

As a Christian father, Mr. Benson knew the perfect example of the Lord Jesus Christ and the high principles taught in the gospel of Christ. A wondrous power is given to those who have grace. The boys' father used this power, along with anxious watching and earnest prayer, to influence and train them. By God's grace, Mr. Benson had successfully worked this power. He could say without boasting, "I have taught my sons to speak the truth. I am sure they will speak the truth."

Charles and Harry did not behave without fault. Their eagerness, combined with a good measure of cheerfulness, sometimes led them into small troubles and difficulties. The boys loved to play practical jokes. Although harmless, the victims of the jokes did not always enjoy them. The neighbors liked the boys very well. Yet if anything unusual happened around Park Villas, the neighbors usually said, "Dear me, those Benson boys are playing their tricks again!"

Mr. Benson, shut up in his study almost all day long, did not know all that went on even in his own house. His neighbors said that they respected him too much to bother him about his boys. Besides, the neighbors regarded Charles and Harry as favorites in spite of their energy. Mr. Arnold, however, did not share in this general feeling.

Mr. Arnold had lived in No. 2 Park Villas for about three years. He was a brisk, active, little elderly man. At one time in his life he had owned a business in the city with which he had made a fortune. How large a fortune I do not know. He had plenty of money, however, for his own wants and some to spare. He had never married, so he had no family to support. Never having had any children of his own made him more unreasonable about other people's children. Why Mr. Arnold had moved into a house with boys for neighbors is unknown. Perhaps he found it difficult to find a neighborhood without a parcel of children. Maybe he congratulated himself that there were only two.

Several contrasts existed between Mr. Arnold and Mr. Benson. One had been married, and the other was a bachelor. Mr. Arnold was rich; Mr. Benson, if not poor, was near poverty. Mr. Arnold had worked hard and was successful for many busy years. Now he could afford to be idle. Mr. Benson worked hard also throughout his life. Yet he still had to continue working hard for his daily bread.

The largest contrast of all was that through faith in the gospel of Jesus Christ, Mr. Benson looked forward to the end of his bodily life on earth. He knew death on earth was the beginning of a spiritual life of perfect happiness in the presence of the God he loved. This faith enabled him to say, "For our light affliction, which is but for a moment, worketh for us a far more exceeding and eternal weight of glory."

Mr. Arnold had very little regard for the gospel and its glorious revelations. Mr. Arnold looked upon the world as the home of his happiness and the limit of his hopes and wishes. He looked to death as a dreary end of life to which he must some day submit. He shrank from death with dismay. You will admit this is an important difference and contrast. I ask whether in this matter, you are more like Mr. Arnold or Mr. Benson?

While Mr. Arnold could afford to be idle, he really was not. He felt so accustomed to active employment that idleness held no charm for him. So having retired from the pleasures as well as the cares and risks of business, he turned his attention to the science that deals with plants. His zeal in this pursuit almost matched in proportion with his ignorance of this science.

A high wall separated the good-sized gardens behind Park Villas. Fruit-bearing trees grew on both sides of the wall. In other respects, however, the two gardens presented a striking contrast. Mr. Benson's boys used his garden as a playground, so it was rough and in disorder. Mr. Arnold kept his garden neatly groomed. It was crowded with plants and shrubs which he especially delighted to raise and watch over.

A few months earlier Mr. Arnold had purchased a wonderful flowering plant unlike any he had seen before. The man from the flower shop gave it the fine Latin name of *Progidium Mundi.* He also told Mr. Arnold the name meant: "the wonder of the world." Perhaps the seller took advantage of the weakness of Mr. Arnold. Whether he did or not the buyer felt pleased with his purchase. Mr. Arnold took special care of the plant when he got it home.

The plant grew and flourished. From a small pot he transferred the plant to a larger pot. From the larger pot eventually he transplanted it into a garden bed. It became the garden's showpiece. Mr. Arnold never tired of looking at it and admiring it. Early in the morning Mr. Arnold walked into his garden to pay a visit to his *Progidium Mundi.* The last gleam of daylight would find him visiting the same spot. He made no secret of his treasure. In fact, being rather a boastful gentleman, he took pride in showing off his plant to his neighbors. (He didn't have any close friends.) He would have felt unhappy to discover that other neighbors could have matched him in this possession. They could not do this, so Mr. Arnold's flowering plant was looked upon as being unique. He felt gratified.

Alas for the uncertainty of all earthly enjoyments or sources of human pride. One morning Mr. Arnold found the pride of his garden laid low. He found the juicy and tender stem of the *Prodigiun Mundi* broken off close to the root, and the gorgeous blossoms already withered and dying, shattered on the ground.

There lay the instrument of destruction—a common stick. It was a bit of wood, fit enough for burning or for pig-driving or for any other degrading use, but …

Ah well, I hope you will sympathize with the distressed gardener's sorrow and respect his indignation. Mr. Arnold raved about his loss until his elderly housekeeper said it was unbearable. He fixed in his own mind who was guilty, and leveled his charge against them as I have already told.

Chapter 2

THE TRUTH IS TOLD

A gentle knock came at the door of No. 2, Park Villas that afternoon. Mr. Benson and his two boys were invited in. "I have brought my sons to see your flower-garden, if you will allow them to do so, Mr. Arnold," said Mr. Benson.

"Oh certainly, Mr. Benson, but what's the use?" said Mr. Arnold sullenly. "Better let the thing drop. Of course, ..."

"Will you have the kindness, Mr. Arnold, not to repeat that, 'of course'? The boys know nothing of what has passed between us. They are wondering why I brought them to you instead of sitting them down to their dinner. I wish you to hear what they have to say with an open mind."

"Very well, Mr. Benson ... very well," said Mr. Arnold, leading the way. "It shall be as you like. But as to ... well ..."

"The bad stick ... where is that, Mr. Arnold?"

Mr. Arnold said he had taken care of that. He had not put it back where he had found it, but could produce it.

"Now, boys," said their father when they had reached the flowerbed and had the remains of the

*"This stick, young gentlemen. This!" interrupted
Mr. Arnold, producing the stick and nervously clutching it.*

Prodigium Mundi in full view. "You see, our neighbor, Mr. Arnold, has had a sad disaster here."

Charles and Harry looked at the ruined plant and then at each other, but they did not speak.

"Mr. Arnold found his favorite plant in this condition this morning. Underneath or close by it, he found a stick ..."

"This stick, young gentlemen. This!" interrupted Mr. Arnold, producing the stick and nervously clutching it.

"Mr. Arnold," continued Mr. Benson, "believes that one of you boys threw the stick causing the damage. I have brought you here to ask you simply if you know anything of the matter."

"There, there, don't say anymore; don't ask them, Mr. Benson. What can't be cured must be endured. It isn't worthwhile. No, it really isn't," said Mr. Arnold hastily. "It is a pity we should be bad neighbors after all, Sir." he added.

"Did either of you throw this stick into Mr. Arnold's garden?" the father asked rather quickly.

"Yes, Father, I did," said Harry turning red, "but I did not mean ... but I did not throw ..."

"I told Harry to throw it," said the elder brother hastily interrupting.

"Why did you throw it?" demanded Mr. Benson of his younger son.

The elder answered for him, "Why, you know, Father, there's a large cat that comes after our young rabbits. He has killed two of them. We sat up to watch last night, and we saw the beast creeping along the top of the wall. Harry had a stick in his hand, so I told him to throw it at her, and he did."

"See what mischief the two of you have done," said the father.

"I am very sorry, Father," said Harry. "We didn't think about Mr. Arnold's flowers, only about our rabbits."

"Your 'not thinking' caused a lot of damage. Besides you disobeyed me, for I have forbidden you to throw either sticks or stones."

"I am very sorry" said Charles. "Father, the fault belongs to me, really. Harry would not have thrown the stick if I hadn't told him to."

"Between the two of you, you have caused unpleasantness between neighbors by destroying Mr. Arnold's property. In addition, you have offended me by your disobedience," said Mr. Benson reproachfully. You can go now," he added.

The two boys left rather embarrassed. They felt sorry that they had offended their father and sorry that they had done mischief. They were not sorry, however, that they had told the truth.

The boys had no fear of being beaten because they had behaved with thoughtless disobedience that resulted in accidental damage. Knowing that they had displeased their father was punishment enough for them. Perhaps a greater punishment still, they knew that because of their thoughtlessness he was suffering disgrace. It never occurred to them to tell a lie, even to escape his displeasure or to shelter him from irritation.

"You see, boys can tell the truth sometimes, Mr. Arnold," said the father when his sons were out of hearing. "But we will not carry on that argument. I have to express my sorrow for the injury done to you. I want to make whatever restoration I can."

"Pooh, pooh! It is not worthwhile to say anything more. Your boys confessed their fault handsomely enough, which was more than I expected. As to compensation, why you know neither you, nor they, nor all the men in Jerusalem can stick my poor *Prodigium* together again. So the least said the soonest mended."

"But I would like to at least pay the value of the plant they destroyed," said Mr. Benson. Better he had not spoken those words, for his neighbor still felt irritated over his loss. Exceeding this irritation, was his mortification at being proved wrong about the boys never behaving with generosity or truthfulness.

Under the smart of his defeat, Mr. Arnold broke out hastily and angrily with, "Pay, Sir! Pay, Mr. Benson! Do you take me for a horse-trader, Sir? Pay indeed! I have money enough, Mr. Benson, and at any rate I don't want any of yours. Money won't undo the mischief will it, Sir?" Mr. Arnold went on for some time raving about the insult which Mr. Benson had given him. Rich man as he was, how could anyone assume that money would cure his trouble? The irritated gentleman complained on and on.

The Bible says, "Seest thou a man that is hasty in his words? There is more home of a fool than of him," Proverbs 29:20. Mr. Benson remembered this proverb, and he wisely refrained from further argument. He felt that anything he could say further would become lost on his unreasoning neighbor. He knew also "in the multitude of words there wanteth not sin." Wishing Mr. Arnold a good day, therefore, Mr. Benson returned to his own house.

He and his two sons only know what passed between them afterwards as they all three took their evening stroll. We can presume that the quarrel was not very violent. Mr. Benson probably felt pleased in his heart that his boys told the truth, even though annoyed at the damage they had done. From that time on Charles and Harry Benson carefully avoided offending their disagreeable, boy-hating neighbor in any way.

As to Mr. Arnold, the injury he had received festered painfully in his heart. At least he fancied that it did. Some people live and thrive upon suffering, grow fat upon it, hug it to their hearts, and will not part with it at any price. Now this was very much the case with Mr. Arnold. He had long lived in wealth and in the enjoyment of having everything his own way. In contrast, a little disappointment and contradiction felt exciting. Excitement being pleasant, he took care to keep the feeling alive.

If this gentleman had sought out real trouble in the world and then attempted to lessen the suffering, he would no doubt have felt happier. He should have understood and received the words of the apostle. "What? Know ye not that your body is the temple of the Holy Ghost which is in you, which ye have of God, and ye are not your own? For ye are bought with a price: therefore glorify God in your body, and in your spirit, which are God's," 1 Corinthians 6:19-20. Then Mr. Arnold would have known that God gave life for higher purposes than to eat, drink, sleep, get rich, and fret about trifles. This verse meant nothing, however, to him. He did not recognize them as being important; therefore, he chose to fret himself about trifles.

I do not mean that suffering a loss, even an unintentional loss, is not annoying. Anyone, even a Christian, would have felt temporarily and justly annoyed to have a rare and favorite plant destroyed. A good and wise Christian, however, would not have brooded over his loss as Mr. Arnold did. He brooded until he received a strange and unnatural sort of gratification in the remembrance of it.

Holding on to his embittered feelings, Mr. Arnold gave his next-door neighbors a rough and short greeting when they came into contact with him. He avoided even this contact as far as he possibly could. The two houses, No. 1 and No. 2, Park Villas, were much like two neighboring countries between which some great misunderstanding had arisen. Any fresh irritation might ripen into active hostility. The two parties had a vast difference in their temper and disposition. The gentleman in No. 2 kept his anger ready prepared to start up on the slightest impulse.

He took a morbid pleasure in leaving a vacant space in his flower-bed where the unfortunate *Prodigium Mundi* had once flourished. His neighbors at No. 1 had humble hearts and would have made many sacrifices to restore friendly feelings.

Several months after the great offense, the boys' uncle, Wallace, who lived a few miles off invited Charles and Harry Benson to spend a few days. While they visited, he gave the two boys permission to ramble over a nursery-ground in the neighborhood. They enjoyed this as well as talking with the friendly owner.

"Charles, Charles! Look here," said the younger brother, stopping short in his stroll through one of the greenhouses. As he spoke, he pointed to a flowering plant on one tier of the shelves.

"What is it, Harry?"

"What is it! Why don't you see it is a *Prodigium Mundi*, just like you-know-whose?" said Harry.

"So it is," said Charles.

"What do you call it, young gentleman?" asked the gardener, with an amused expression on his face.

"*Prodigium Mundi*, Sir, isn't that the right name?" Harry asked.

"I never heard it called by that name," replied the nurseryman, smiling.

"Never mind what it is called; that's our name for it," said Charles.

"I wonder," he whispered to Harry. "I wonder whether we could buy it. Is it very expensive, Sir?" he asked the nurseryman in a louder tone.

"That depends pretty much upon what you mean by expensive," the owner answered.

"I really don't know, Sir," said Charles. Then he asked, "Is it an uncommon flower, Sir?"

"Not now. Two years ago when first introduced, the plant sold for a guinea."

"O...oh!" said Harry drawing in his breath. "That was expensive then."

"Last year the plant was not as rare because more plants grew from cuttings. Then a single plant sold for half-a-guinea. Now," continued the gardener, "a new plant sells for five shillings."

"Let us buy it and take it home to Mr. Arnold," said Charles. "He bought his about this time of year, you know."

Harry put his hand in his pocket and pulled out his money. He did not have much. After the two brothers combined their funds and paid for the plant, neither had much left.

"What do you plan to do with the plant, young gentlemen?" asked the nurseryman. He had watched the boys work out their finances with amusement.

"Take it with us, Sir, when we go home," Charles said.

"Yes, and what then, if I may ask?"

"Well Sir, we shall give it to a gentleman who lives close by our house," said Harry. "You know, Sir ... you don't know, but we do, that he had a fine

Prodig ... I mean, a plant like this, growing in his garden last summer. I had the misfortune to break it right at the stem and so ..."

"And so you plan to give him this instead. Very good! I should think the gentleman will feel pleased with you. Since you are paying for the plant with your own money, I would like to help you out a little. I cannot afford to give my stock-in-trade away, but I can do this." The good-natured nurseryman put back a shilling into each of the boys' hands. "No, never mind about thanking me. It is all right. How did you come by the name *Prodigium Mundi*, young gentlemen?"

"That's what Mr. Arnold called it," said Charles. "And so did the man he bought the plant from."

"The man pulled a joke, I suspect, and your friend was rather gullible. You may tell him that the name of the plant is Bledstraw. If he wants to keep it through the winter, he should cover it up from frosts."

Charles and Harry felt pleased to bring home the plant they had purchased. They thought the plant would calm Mr. Arnold at last. Once more peace would reign between Park Villas, No. 1 and No. 2.

As Mr. Arnold ate breakfast on the following morning, the peace-offering reached him accompanied by a short note which said:

Dear Sir,

Will you please accept a plant for your flower-bed? We think it is just like that which we ruined last summer, only not as large. We hope it will grow when transplanted. We hope you will accept our apologies for the mischief we unintentionally did. We hope we can all become good friends in the future. The person we got the plant from tells us that the name of it is not Prodigium Mundi, but Bledstraw. He says that it can survive winters outdoors if protected from frosts.

Yours very respectfully,
Charles and Harry Benson

The brothers and their father hoped that this note and the present would wipe out all unkindness from the thoughts of Mr. Arnold. How sad and troubled they felt when within the half hour Mr. Arnold returned the poor plant. He also requested that the Bensons send him no more messages. The unhappy gentleman became more enraged than ever by the attempt to make amends. Mr. Arnold was very vain of his wealth and scornful of his neighbor's poorer circumstances. He looked upon it as an insult that he should receive a gift from people he considered lesser than he. Worse even than this, he was embarrassed at having his ignorance innocently exposed and set right by boys. Acting from his unhappy pride and ill-temper, Mr. Arnold hung on to his grudge against his neighbors.

"We cannot help it, boys," said Mr. Benson to his sons when he saw their faces covered with disappointment. "You have done what you could to win back Mr. Arnold to being a friendly neighbor. Now we must let the matter rest. It is a pity," he added. "Mr. Arnold has such a strange temper. I am sure it is a cause of much sorrow to him."

Not long after this occurrence the Bensons moved from No. 1, Park Villas to another neighborhood. In their new home they soon forgot the petty annoyances they had experienced from Mr. Arnold or remembered them only with a smile. As to Mr. Arnold, he soon found there may be more unpleasant next-door neighbors than even "a parcel of boys."

Chapter 3

THE TRUTH IS REWARDED

"I'll do it," said Mr. Arnold to himself. "That is, I have a good mind to do it," he added softening his first rather rash determination.

"Let me see," he went on. "There is a little risk to run, certainly. I did know a young fellow once who worked in a bank and managed to steal some money. In this case, however, I don't think there is much risk. The boy's father brought him up well. He could tell the truth when a lie would have answered his purpose better at the time. I owe him something for what he did afterwards. Yes, I'll step out of my way for once and do it."

Not spoken aloud, these words passed through Mr. Arnold's thoughts as he rode on a bus returning from the city. About four or five years had passed since he had seen his former neighbors of No. 1, Park Villas.

Changes had come over Mr. Arnold in these years. Not great changes, nor sudden changes, but many almost unnoticeable changes because they were so slow. The first change was that as he had grown older, he had become more feeble. Why it

25

was he could not understand, for he was only sixty-five years of age. He felt troubled by the changes in himself. At sixty, Mr. Arnold was active. He was not only fond of exercise but capable of strain. At sixty-five, he was sluggish and soon tired. He could not account for the difference. It could not be his age he thought, for what was sixty-five?

Five years before he had taken pleasure and pride in his garden. He had spaded, raked, sown, and planted. Now he did not care a bit about it. It had become too hard for him to do the necessary work. He employed a gardener to come to work the garden, but that made his ground cost twice as much as it was worth. So Mr. Arnold came to the conclusion that a garden was an annoyance and expense.

A change had taken place in his household. He had fought with his housekeeper. She had left him in anger. He filled her place with another. This change was neither for the better nor for the worse. Mr. Arnold had little regard for housekeepers except as being necessary burdens.

A change had taken place in Mr. Arnold's next door neighbors as we have already seen. Many changes, in fact, had taken place. No. 1, Park Villas had had three tenants since it lost Mr. Benson. These changes had seriously affected the temper of the tenant of No. 2. Every tenant of No. 1 was, in Mr. Arnold's mind, worse than the previous one.

The first of the three neighbors had a large family of small children. With the ceaseless noise they made at all hours of the day in the adjoining garden, he could have no peace. There was one comfort, however; they went to bed early. This left him some quiet hours in the evening until his bed-time.

The next tenant, in addition to having children, owned a noisy dog. Chained up at night, the dog kept awake the whole neighborhood with its howls, and thus disturbed Mr. Arnold's sleep. This tenant moved, saving Mr. Arnold the trouble of taking the legal action he had threatened.

To Mr. Arnold's comfort the next tenant had neither children or dog. Alas! The comfort was short-lived. This new neighbor had a bad practice of keeping a lot of noisy company two or three nights in the week. Wild drunken songs and roars of laughter which resounded through the thin walls destroyed the troubled gentleman's rest. Added to this, the neighbor's wife had a very shrill voice and uncertain temper. Her chief employment through the day seemed to be that of scolding two unhappy servants. Mr. Arnold felt almost driven to desperation. He thought about moving from his house into a new neighborhood. He worried, however, that wherever he might go he would not be out of reach of either children, dogs, "jolly companions," or scolds.

Mr. Arnold's health as well as comfort had suffered from his later disagreeable neighbors. He looked back with regret to the time when the quiet Bensons were the tenants of No. 1. He felt remorse when he remembered how disagreeably he had behaved to them.

A change had also taken place with regard to the future destination of his riches. I have said that it did not appear that Mr. Arnold had any very attached friends. In truth he had passed through life without making a single friendship. At the age when friendships are usually made, he was too much engrossed in making money. He had not many relatives and had outlived the few he had known in his youth. When he was sixty years old, one person remained whom Mr. Arnold recognized as being of his kin. A person whom he had never seen, a village schoolmaster unmarried like himself. He had settled in his mind that this person would become the sole inheritor of his wealth; not that Mr. Arnold liked looking forward to that coming time.

Now a few years after making that decision, he was disagreeably reminded of the unavoidable fact of dying. His far-off cousin had died. On the day he returned from the city on the bus, he still wore black around his hat for his cousin. He had not yet decided about the future destination of his growing wealth. The change which death had made was very distasteful to Mr. Arnold and made him feel gloomy.

Therefore, I fear that amid all the changes this old gentleman had experienced, he had not felt the important change of heart which alone can remove terror from the thought of dying. In this respect Mr. Arnold was the same at sixty-five as he had been at sixty. Not to dwell upon this, however, we return to the point from which we just now started.

"I have a mind to do it," said Mr. Arnold to himself as he returned from the city.

Mr. Arnold's mind had received a great shock in the city...or what was to him a great shock. He had gone to his bank and a friend, one of the partners in the bank, had taken him aside.

"Excuse my troubling you, Mr. Arnold, but do you happen to know anything of a Benson family?"

"Benson? Well yes, I had some slight knowledge of a Mr. Benson some years ago. That is to say, he lived next door to me."

"Exactly so, at No. 1, Park Villas. Your address is No.2, I know, of course."

"Ah, then it must be the same Benson. Why do you ask?"

"I'll tell you presently, but let us make sure first. My Mr. Benson...that is, the person I mean...was a writer. He had something to do with the public press," said the banker.

"So had mine," replied Mr. Arnold.

"And he had two sons, being himself a widower," continued the banker.

"True. The person I knew was a widower and had two sons," Mr. Arnold responded.

"Must be the same. Well, the poor man is dead," said the banker.

"Dead! Dear, dear! Why he was a young man twenty years younger than myself, I should say," observed Mr. Arnold quite unstrung.

"Excuse my troubling you, Mr. Arnold, but do you happen to know anything of a Benson family?"

"My good Sir, we have found in our experience that younger men than we sometimes suddenly die," remarked the banker.

"True, Sir, true, but we don't seem to expect it either. It makes us feel rather down when we hear it of those we have known. You said suddenly too, Sir. Did he die very suddenly?" asked Mr. Arnold.

"Quite suddenly about two months ago. This is not the worst of it. Sadly for those he left behind, he died poor also," said the banker.

"I am not surprised, not surprised at all, Sir," said Mr. Arnold. "Of course he was poor; I always thought so. Never heard of a man in such a profession getting right, Sir. The greater fools they are for going into it."

"Possibly, my good friend, but we need not enter upon that question," said the banker musingly.

"You knew Mr. Benson then, Sir?" Mr. Arnold asked.

"Not personally. I have read some of his writings ('That's more than I have,' thought Mr. Arnold.) and that has given me a sort of acquaintance with him. This brings me to the matter at hand. One of the sons has been recommended to me as a clerk. I have seen the lad and like his looks. I have examined his abilities and find that he is well educated, but..." and here the banker paused.

"Which of the boys is it, Sir?" asked Mr. Arnold in a tone which seemed to say that he had no particular interest in the matter.

"The younger, his name is Henry or Harry, I don't know which. The elder boy is in some place of business in the city, I hear."

"Oh, and you wish ..." began Mr. Arnold.

"I wish to know what you think of the younger boy. You saw something of him, I daresay, when he lived next door to you. I may as well tell you that your name was mentioned by chance when I questioned him of his past. He hesitated, which I thought betrayed that you knew something about him which he would prefer not to become known."

Now I have said or implied that Mr. Arnold was a testy and conceited person, but he was not spiteful and harmful. Moreover, he would have shrunk from anything dishonorable in the way of business. Add to this his late guilt-filled memories of his old neighbors and the shock he had just received in hearing of Mr. Benson's sudden death.

Then you will not wonder that he replied promptly, "Not at all, Sir, not at all, I assure you. Boys will be boys, you know. The young Bensons were not men, but for boys they were about the best behaved I ever knew. We had our little spats sometimes, but I declare I was as much at fault as they. I can assure you, as far as I know, I can recommend young Benson with confidence." Mr. Arnold said this very stoutly for it was the truth. The more stoutly, perhaps, that he risked nothing by saying it.

"I am glad to hear it," said the banker. "So far, then, I feel satisfied."

"I hope the young fellow will turn out well," continued Mr. Arnold. "When does he start his new duties?" he asked.

"Well, the desk is vacant for him now. It's too bad that there is still a little hitch."

"Oh!" exclaimed Mr. Arnold.

"Mr. Arnold, we never hire a clerk, however promising his qualities seem, without security against any losses from dishonesty. That's an ugly word to use, of course, but it is best to be plain. Although the young man's friends are respectable, they are not particularly wealthy. We would not feel justified in taking the personal bond of his guardian alone. Yet, I feel an interest in the lad. If anyone else would join in the undertaking, it would do away with the difficulty."

"There is some risk, then?" asked Mr. Arnold.

"Very little, for the few years the bond would cover. It is, in fact, little more than a matter of form. It is a form, however, we do not feel justified leaving out," replied the banker.

"You mention this to me ..." Mr. Arnold paused. The pause implied, "What have I to do with it? Why do you bore me with it?" While he did not utter these questions, the smart man of business understood them.

The banker began, "It struck me, Mr. Arnold, that as an old friend of the young man's father ..."

"No, no, not a friend particularly, that is going too far," Mr. Arnold said hastily.

"Well, knowing him and having expressed a good opinion of the son, you might not object to joining in the bond."

"Never did such a thing in my life," said Mr. Arnold. Then he added more hastily, "Never was security for anybody. Always set myself dead against it."

"Oh well, if you object that ends the matter," said the banker. "I wished to do the lad a kindness for his father's sake as well as his own. If I cannot, however, I cannot."

Mr. Arnold went his way, but he could not dismiss the suggestion from his thoughts. He remembered the time, now fifty years ago, when he was a lonely and poor youth. A friend had taken his hand and helped him over some stumbling blocks that lay in the way of his success in life. He thought with some regret that he had never put himself out of the way to help any other struggling youth. After much thought, Mr. Arnold came to the conclusion, "Yes, I'll step out of my way, for once, and do it."

He did it. I am afraid not without some worry over the evil results of departing from the rule of his life. However, he did it. He returned to the city on the following day and put his name to the bond. A few days afterwards, Harry Benson took his seat at the vacant desk and became a banker's clerk.

At the age of sixty-five years, Mr. Arnold experienced a new sensation. He had put himself out of the way to be kind. At first he felt somewhat doubtful about the possible outcome of his rash act.

He had a few restless nights thinking about what a blow he would receive if the new banker's clerk proved unworthy of his trust. After a time he got over these uncomfortable feelings. Especially when his banker friend told him that young Benson performed well at his new job. His employers found him to be steady, useful, and trustworthy. After this, Mr. Arnold enjoyed the luxury of thinking how nice he was to have given the young fellow a helping-hand.

*"You remember my Prodigium Mundi, I daresay,
or perhaps you have forgotten all about it."*

Chapter 4

A FRIENDSHIP GROWS

As one of the results of Mr. Arnold's helpful kindness to Harry Benson, he began to take an interest in the youth. This was strange for him, for he had never before taken much interest in any human being.

"I think I will ask young Benson to come to see me some evening," said Mr. Arnold to himself. "I daresay he will like to see his old home again."

He sent the invitation and Harry accepted. One summer's evening Harry made his appearance at No. 2, Park Villas.

"Really," thought Mr. Arnold, during the evening, "he is a nice, intelligent lad. He is not like the same boy that worried me so five years ago."

"Really," thought Harry Benson, at about the same instant, "Mr. Arnold is a very pleasant old gentleman. He is not at all like the disagreeable grouch we thought him five years ago. I have forgotten to thank him for giving his security. I'll do it now."

"It was very kind and generous for you to pay for the bond, Sir," he said. "Especially as, I had no kind of claim upon you."

"I don't know about claim, Harry, but there was a reason. You remember my *Prodigium Mundi*, I daresay, or perhaps you have forgotten all about it."

"No Sir, indeed," returned Harry, blushing. "I remember it very well. I remember that I behaved like a mischievous young boy at that time, although I didn't mean to. I am afraid that my brother and I caused you a lot of annoyance."

"A little, now and then, not worth speaking about or thinking of now. There's one thing you didn't do. You did not tell a lie to hide your faults. That's the reason I mentioned it, Harry," said Mr. Arnold.

"Was it so strange to you, Sir, that I ... that we, my brother and I, should prefer speaking the truth to telling a lie?" Harry asked.

"Yes ... well, yes, it did seem strange, Harry," said Mr. Arnold. "Right or wrong, I had believed until then that all boys are natural liars. So you must not mind when I say that I classed you both as liars."

"No Sir, I don't mind that, although I am sorry you had such an opinion of boys in general," returned the young man.

"Well, I had. To tell you the truth, when I found out my mistake, I felt more distressed than pleased, for it made me look like a fool. Anyway, I thought it did after what I said to your father. This is partly why I treated you so badly afterwards when you made me that handsome present which I refused to accept."

"Do not say anymore about it, Sir," said Harry.

Mr. Arnold said, "Well, I won't say much more, only that I have thought about it a good deal in one way and another since that time. When I had a chance to do that little thing for you ..."

"Ah Sir, it was not a little thing to me, I assure you," Harry could not help saying gratefully.

"So much the better, Harry. At any event, when the banker suggested I do it, I said to myself ... a boy or a man who won't tell a lie is safe. He can't be dishonest. That's all there is to it, Harry."

Harry Benson enjoyed his visit with Mr. Arnold, and Mr. Arnold enjoyed Harry's company. As a result many other visits followed. When looking forward to the anticipated pleasure of the young man's visits, Mr. Arnold halfway forgot to become annoyed by his noisy neighbors at No. 1.

By-and-by, Mr. Arnold remembered that Harry Benson had a brother. "Why don't you bring him down with you?" he asked one evening.

Nothing would give Harry more pleasure if he might do so, he said, and so he invited his brother Charles.

If Mr. Arnold felt pleased with Harry, he felt equally pleased with the elder brother. Now another new idea stole over him. He had lived alone all his life. The pursuit of making money had taken up much of his time and thoughts, so much that he had not realized what a lonely and joyless life he was leading. For the last ten years a growing belief had taken hold of his mind. He began to believe that having money was not the only thing necessary to being happy. He had heard and read about the pleasures and blessings of social and family life. Well, he could not begin life again. To attempt beginning over, now that he was more than sixty-five years old, was absurd.

Was it equally absurd to think that he might in part obtain, for the remaining years of his life, some of the pleasures which he had so long missed? He thought not. Here he was a lonely man without home, companion, or son to cheer his old age. Here were two youths whose company had stirred up these regrets in his mind. "They have no father; I have no sons. Let them live with me instead of spending their evenings in lonely lodgings," thought Mr. Arnold.

Mr. Arnold made the proposal. After much hesitation on the part of Charles and Harry, they decided to give the suggestion a try. "You can leave me when you get tired of me," said Mr. Arnold on the first evening. "I will not complain if you should soon tire of me."

They said, "Agreed."

Ten years have passed since then, and now Mr. Arnold is truly an old man. He still lives at No. 2 but not alone. The young man Harry Benson, who first awakened in his heart the feelings of human compassion, still lives with him. He still retains his bank clerkship but spends his evenings, mornings, and holidays in No. 2, Park Villas, his home.

Pass into the garden and you will see a choice collection of flowers in bed, border, and ornamental baskets all kept in the nicest order. The old man's fondness for flowers has returned to him now that he has a friend to share his enjoyment with.

"And that very brilliant and luxuriant flowering plant which seems to be the pride of your garden, Sir, and of which you seem to have so many varieties, will you kindly tell us the name?"

Old Mr. Arnold genially smiles as he replies, "*Prodigium Mundi*, I call it. It is not the right name, of course, but it always goes by that name here."

New neighbors now live at No. 1 next door. Five years have passed since the noisy, company-keeping gentleman and his scolding wife moved from the neighborhood. After that came another tenant who lived quietly, for he had neither children nor dog nor loud, night-loving friends. The tenant did not take kindly to Park Villas, however, and when his three years' lease had expired, he moved.

No. 1 did not remain unoccupied for long. A young married couple presently live there. The husband is junior partner in a business in the city. The tenants of Nos. 1 and 2 share a special friendship and harmony. They visit each other very frequently. Mr. Arnold has proposed opening a doorway in the wall that separates their gardens. This would save him the trouble of descending and ascending the front-door steps leading to the two houses. The name of the young married man at No. 1 is Charles Benson.

Let us listen now to a few words of conversation. It is a fine sunny, spring afternoon. The young wife of Charles Benson is in the garden of No. 2 with her husband's aged friend Mr. Arnold. He walks slowly by her side, half supported by her stronger arm, while she adjusts her pace to his.

"My husband and I have very good reason to feel grateful to you, Mr. Arnold," the lady is saying. "Without your help, Charles's old employers would not have taken him into partnership. Then, you know, we could not have married for I don't know how long," she adds with a blush.

"My dear Caroline," replies the aged companion, "you think too much of that matter. The truth is, I have lost nothing, but I am a gainer by investing a thousand pounds as I did. It pays me better interest. What I have wanted to say to you is that I am under far greater debt to your husband and his brother than they can ever be to me."

"It is kind of you to say so, Sir."

"It is only honest to say so, my dear lady. You will listen to me, I know, for you do not object to hearing an old man's chatter. I will give you a short history.

"When I entered business life more than sixty years ago, I met a good many difficulties. I had to bear a large amount of abuse. I had one friend, however, who helped me out of my troubles. He gave me the start in life which led on to future success. Success, which I now can see I did not at all deserve."

"You worked hard for it, I have no doubt, Mr. Arnold," the lady interposes.

"Yes, I worked hard early and late and almost without stopping. I worked for myself, however, and myself only. I had no thought beyond myself. I could not show gratitude to the friend who had given me the needed help because he died before the results of his kindness had ripened. I did not consider myself under the least duty to anyone else. I became selfish and grasping, my dear. More than that, I gradually lost the little faith I ever had in the people around me. I became deceived, I must say this for myself. If I had not been, I would not have become what I am now, an old bachelor. I felt cheated out of my life's happiness, so I looked upon it as fair play to distrust everybody I had to deal with. Can you understand this, my dear?"

The lady replied, "Partly, I can, at least I think I can. I can sympathize with you, Sir."

"Thank you heartily. You encourage me to go on with my confessions. I will not trouble you with all my history, but after a time, I began to save money. I don't believe I was ever a miser, Caroline. I like money well enough for its conveniences, but I did not fall in love with it and hoard it for its own sake. It gave me power though. I like that, and I like to show my power. I can see now as I look back upon my business life that I must have been a disagreeable and overbearing employer. I never won confidence and respect from my employees. They served me, I have no doubt, more from self-interest and fear than from love. No wonder that I saw the worst side of human character. At any rate I did see a bad side of it. I became even more sure that I could expect neither truth nor honesty from anyone.

"I kept on getting money, however. When I thought I had enough or perhaps felt afraid that if I went on much longer in business I would lose what I had made, I retired. I came to live here.

"I brought with me all my former prejudices and my old habit of expecting everyone around me to bend to my will. I also had a special dislike towards young people ... boys in particular. I cannot exactly explain this, my dear, but I have sometimes thought that this feeling arose from envy. Whatever the cause, I vented this feeling of spite on the two boys who lived next door. I did not like them ... not for any harm they had done me nor for any annoyance they caused, but just because they were boys. Very shocking to hear this, is it not, Caroline?"

"It must have felt unpleasant to you to have such feelings, Mr. Arnold," the lady observes.

"You are right; it was unpleasant. I became my own tormentor, as is the case with all ill-tempered people. There is no doubt of that. My dislike was sinful as well. I did not know that then, and perhaps would not have cared much if I had known.

"To go on with my history, I come to that trifling affair ... the destruction of my flower ... my *Prodigium Mundi,* as I called it," says the old gentleman with a smile on his face.

"As we all call it now," adds the lady.

"Yes, as you all call it to humor an old man's fancy. Well, it is *Prodigium Mundi* to me, my dear, and something more. For that incident, foolish and ridiculous as it may seem to anyone else, became to me a most blessed event. It was the first dawning of a new light into my mind, my dear."

Mr. Arnold pauses here and walks on a few steps in silence. Then he resumes his story.

"You have heard all about that little affair, I know. I will only tell you, Caroline, that the straightforward way of truthfulness shown by those two boys ... one of them your husband now ... first took me by surprise. It almost enraged me at the time, for I had made up my mind that they would deny the deed. I thought they would defy me with protests of innocence. Yet, afterwards I admired their honesty."

"But surely, Sir," the lady remarks, "boys speaking the truth was not so unusual. Even though they might have saved themselves trouble by lying."

"It seemed unusual to me, dear lady. Remember what I have told you ... I had no faith in anyone," said Mr. Arnold.

"You had no faith in yourself, Mr. Arnold?" asked the lady.

"Ha! I see what you mean. Well, I had this sort of faith in myself. I had discovered during a long and busy life that over time honesty is the best policy. So I had the habit of being pretty true. I am afraid that my worldly integrity, such as it was, never had a higher origin. It had never prevented my distrusting every person with whom I had any dealings."

"Not a happy disposition, Sir," the lady says.

"Anything but a happy disposition, believe me," the old gentleman replies promptly. "Happy or unhappy, so it was with me. As I tell you, the straightforward and frank truthfulness of those two boys struck me as something very strange and unaccountable. My good friend," he adds with emotion, "you have a darling baby as yet unaware of evil. Let your first lessons ... your first teaching ... be truth. Make the dear child understand that this is the foundation of every other virtue; there can be no virtue without truth."

"With God's help, I will do this," says the lady fervently.

"I know you will. Yet, I could not help speaking. Now to take up my story once more, I secretly admired those two boys for their honesty. I also envied their father of the treasure he possessed in them. Yet, my pride and conceit prevented my making any amends for my first impressions about them. It led me to reject their offers of peace.

"You know what followed, my dear. The boys and their father disappeared. The next I heard of them five years later, the father had died and the younger boy wanted a job. In those five years, Caroline, I had found out partly, only partly, how hollow and truthless and without purpose my life was. I had begun to look uncomfortably towards the future. I had gone on and on through life pretty well satisfied with myself. Now I began to wonder what the end would be or where it would end. I could not bear to think of death. Yet, sometimes I felt compelled to think of it. Do you understand this feeling?"

"I believe I do, Sir. Where the sting of death remains, the thought of dying is terrible," the lady remarks thoughtfully.

"Yes, as it should, let people try as they may to conceal it, it still feels frightening. It is a wretched state, Caroline, to live in ... as the apostle describes it ... 'having no hope and without God in the world.' Well I had received a shock when my cousin died. That shock was repeated when I heard of the death of your husband's father. I feel that this tamed me down. It made me more willing to atone for my past bad behavior toward the boys when the chance came my way.

"You know what followed. First Harry came to see me and then Harry's brother. The more I saw of them the better I liked them. That is too mild a word: I began to love them. I began to think how blessed I would be if those two young men were my own sons. Then the thought came into my mind ... why should they not become sons to me? At last I persuaded them to come to live with me, dear Caroline. That was the beginning of better days for me. Your husband first found out how ... ah! it did not require much finding out ... how empty I was of any religion, although I kept up a mock respect to its form. He found out too how unhappy I felt, though I tried to hide it.

"Well, my dear, one evening when we sat together your dear husband began to tell me of his trials. He told how, in the thickest of them, all his strong faith in Christ supported him. He also told me about his father's illness and death. He shared how his father's faith enabled him to bear all his pains and to look forward to a joyful resurrection. His last words were, 'though I walk through the valley of the shadow of death, I will fear no evil: for thou art with me; thy rod and thy staff they comfort me.' Why do I tell you all this when you have heard the same account from your husband's lips?"

The lady said, "Yes, I have. I have admired the Christian composure shown by his father and the unshaken firmness of his faith."

Mr. Arnold continued, "I also thought it wonderful and strange, and I told your husband so. This, I suppose, was what he wanted. He put the question to me then very kindly but very pointedly, I thought ... whether my religion would stand the test of a dying hour. He dealt very faithfully with me, my dear. Yet, I could not feel offended with him. Although, I tried hard to be, yes, indeed I did.

His words fastened on my mind, and I could not rest."

"You found rest at last, Sir," the lady added.

"I found rest at last, my dear. For your husband led me on, step by step, until I found myself, almost without knowing it, at the feet of the blessed Saviour seeking rest in Him. Then, late in life, I found how true those words are, 'Come unto Me, all ye that labour and are heavy laden, and I will give you rest.' I found that He is able to save all who come to God by Him. The teaching of God's Holy Spirit led me, my dear, to the Lord Jesus Christ; I do not doubt that. Your husband was the gentle, kind and faithful instrument in the Holy Spirit's hand that helped me make use of His means of grace."

"And now, my dear lady," continued the aged speaker, "do you wonder that I am thankful that God, in His wisdom, brought us together? I feel the debts I am under to your husband and his brother are so great that they can never be repaid. Think how they have cheered me in my loneliness, how they opened to me a new life and a new world. Think of how the Spirit used them to teach me, and how all the hopes I have of future eternal happiness have sprung out of my acquaintance with them! My dear," added Mr. Arnold with strong emotion, "do not say anymore of your husband's debts to me. Nothing that I have done or can do is more than a slight return and a very unworthy response to what he has done for me."

"It all sprang," we hear Mr. Arnold say, as his voice dies in the distance. "It all sprang and had its rise in that lesson which those boys learned first at a mother's knee. Afterwards their father instilled the lesson into them by example. They learned to put the lesson into practice from the highest and noblest motives received from Him, who is Himself 'the way, the truth and the life.' I was still a selfish old man ready to die in my sin, and the Lord used their truthfulness as the instrument in His hand to bring me to know the One who said, 'I am the way, the truth, and the life.'"

Part 2:

Little Mary's
First and Last Falsehood

Both children became quite excited with their work.

Little Mary's
First And Last Falsehood

Chapter 1

LISTENING TO SATAN'S DECEITFUL VOICE

"Let's go out," said Charles one fine summer morning to his little sister Mary. "I'm tired of staying in the house. Shall we go and play with the hay in the yard?"

Little Mary willingly agreed to go. The children soon found their way to the hay yard where they had permission to play.

For some time they amused themselves most happily making nests in the hay and throwing it over each other. They chattered all the time as merry little children do. At last Charles proposed that they make one large stack of all the hay, "to show Papa and Mama what they could do." No sooner said than begun. The children worked hard at heaping up the hay by armfuls on one spot. They worked until their haystack became so large and high that they could not reach the top to add more to it. This brought an end to their work. Charles did not like this, for he did not like to give up what he had once begun. He stood for some time looking at their unfinished work, making vain efforts to add a little more to the pile.

Finally Charles pointed to some pitchforks which the children's parents had forbidden them to touch. "Oh, Mary," he said, "if only I could take one of those nice pitchforks, I'd finish our haystack in a few minutes."

"Papa says we are not strong enough to use them properly," replied little Mary. "I'm sure I couldn't for I can hardly lift them."

"Oh, but you're a girl, Mary," answered her brother, "and two years younger than I am, so of course you cannot." Seizing a pitchfork and lifting it over his head, Charles added, "But see how well I can manage one."

Once Charles held the pitchfork in his hands, he could not resist the temptation of putting a few finishing touches to the haystack. Seeing the stack grow bigger and bigger every minute pleased Mary too. She did not urge her brother to put down the forbidden thing as she ought to have. Instead Mary busied herself collecting the hay in heaps for Charles to pitch on the haystack. Both children became quite excited with their work. They worked hard to make the haystack a mountain in height and bulk. Suddenly, their labors came to a sad and unexpected conclusion. Charles stuck his fork into a large heap of hay. He did not realize that his little sister stooped behind it. One of the sharp iron

"Why, how did this happen my child?" said her father.

points of the fork struck the poor little girl in the face just below her right eye.

The blow was so violent that it knocked the child down and stunned her for a few seconds. As the point had struck her just on the cheekbone and not in the eye, it fortunately did not go in far or make a very bad wound. Tears of pain and fright, mingled with the blood from the wound, trickled down poor Mary's cheeks. Charles felt grieved that his disobedience caused the accident which wounded his sister. He tried to comfort her and stop her sobs as he wiped the wounded cheek with his handkerchief. Just then their father passed through the yard. He heard Mary crying and turned back to find out why.

"Oh Papa," said Charles pointing to Mary's bloody cheek, "she has hurt herself very badly."

"Why, how did this happen my child?" said her father. He turned her face to the light and examined the wound. "This is indeed a bad wound."

Neither of the children volunteered any explanation of what happened until their father asked a second time how the accident happened. Satan, the great enemy of truth, diligently used those few seconds of hesitation. He whispered a falsehood into the boy's heart, suggesting to conceal Charles' disobedience. When he did answer, Charles hastily said that Mary had run against the sharp point of the door-latch as she went out the door.

"You must be mistaken, Charles," said his father as he turned around and looked at the door. "Mary can hardly reach the latch with her hand. She could not have hurt her cheek against it."

The boy glanced at the door too and then back again at his sister. "I thought she said so," he answered at length, "but, of course, it could not have happened that way. How did you say you got hurt, Mary?" he continued turning again to the little girl. "Was it against the corner of this big iron-bound chest? You laid close to it when I picked you up."

Mary looked quite surprised at her brother for an instant. She saw no signs of shame in his face; he only frowned and looked sternly at her. She feared to tell the truth because then her father would know about Charles' deceit and his disobedience. Thus, the little girl sobbed out a confirmation to her brother's untruth. Then hiding her face in her hands, she cried louder than before.

Their kind papa sent Mary to the house to get the wounded cheek attended to. Little did he imagine that his children had so grossly deceived him. Charles' pretended innocence had given his father the idea that the accident had not happened in his presence. The father thought his son's first account of it was a misunderstanding of Mary's story. It would have grieved him had he known the truth. How sad he would have felt not only at the boy's double falsehood, but at the boldness and readiness with which he had spoken.

Charles and Mary's parents always tried to teach their children that the fear of the Lord was the only source of true happiness. They sought to train them in the way they should go, so when they grew older, they might not depart from it. They knew that the Word of God, with all its sweet and purifying influences, was the one thing needed to enable them to train their children right. These loving parents daily tried to teach their little ones the things so necessary to their happiness on earth and their eternal salvation hereafter.

Charles caused his parents continual anxiety. Their prayers and efforts on his behalf as yet seemed ineffective. The good seed sown in a child's heart and watered daily by their parents' tears, however, does not often prove unfruitful. It may long lie dormant, but sooner or later our merciful God will cause it to spring up and bear precious fruit, "thirty, sixty, or a hundred fold." Now Charles' conduct would have filled his father's heart with grief and anxiety for the child's future. Yet in later years when the boy grew into an adult, he walked faithfully in "the narrow way." He was the joy and comfort of his parents' hearts.

We shall return to our story, however. Although only a nine year old, Charles was a school-boy. Like many of his companions, he had learned to consider a falsehood almost excusable at times. While Charles congratulated himself on getting out of such a pinch, let us peek into little Mary's heart as she went to the house.

Grief over her sin, her first deliberate falsehood, caused tears to keep trickling down her cheeks. The pain she still felt in her bruised and bleeding cheek did not cause the tears. Mary knew quite well the seriousness of her offense both against God and her kind parents. Still, the fear of her brother's anger and the punishment they deserved laid heavier on her than her sorrow for the sin she had committed. Although she wept as she said it, Mary gave her mother the false account of the accident in answer to her questions as to how she got hurt. Mary's mother gently washed and dressed her wound, but every touch was a fresh prick to the child's sore conscience.

The kindness of the parent she deceived cut her to the very heart. Several times Mary felt tempted to hide her face in her mother's lap and confess the whole truth. She resisted God's Spirit in such a time, promising herself she would never tell another untruth. In this way she tried to soothe her troubled conscience. She decided to say no more about the accident.

Why did little Mary resist the Holy Spirit of God that urged her to show her real sorrow for her sin by immediate confession of it?

Because, my little readers, Satan whispered into her heart that now the thing was done, so she had better let it alone. "Your mother," said this voice, "does not suspect you in the least. Charles would not likely mention his trickery. In fact, you would be a little tattletale to tell on him; it was so much more his fault than yours."

Charles and Mary both received an invitation to a large children's party for the next day. Mary knew that if she told, their parents would not allow Charles to attend the party and that would make her feel bad. "It surely could make no difference now to wait until after tomorrow to tell the truth." Thus reasoned this subtle tempter. Little Mary, as she dried her eyes and sat down to her work, listened to his deceitful voice and remained silent.

*Her bruised and bandaged cheek soon
attracted the attention of her little friends.*

Chapter 2

MARY'S SCARRED CONSCIENCE

As the children awoke the next morning, they saw with delight that the sun shone with unclouded splendor. They planned to spend today with some little friends in the country. A cloudy sky or wet day would have put a damper on their pleasure.

After breakfast, their kind mother helped them dress suitably. After many kisses and wishing them a pleasant day, she saw them safely seated in their papa's carriage and driven away. As she watched them going down the avenue, she wondered why her little Mary's face did not shine with the anticipated pleasure. An expression had clouded over Mary's face that morning that she did not understand.

You could likely have explained the mystery, for you must know that Mary's conscience would not give her much peace until she confessed her sin and deception. At the last moment with her bonnet on and her gloves in her hand, Mary hesitated at the door. The best part of her wanted to tell the truth and give up the party as the punishment she knew she deserved. A glance at her brother already seated in the carriage and flourishing the whip with boyish glee made her decide again to keep her silence.

Thus it often is, little children; the tempter makes our love for others and our misguided kindness to them the means by which he induces us to commit sin. His argument again sealed the little girl's lips. He persuaded her that she would do a most unkind thing to tell the truth because that would bring punishment upon her brother. Mary comforted herself with repeating this reasoning over and over as she rode along. At last cheered by the fresh air, the rapid drive, and her brother's chatter, her usual gayety returned. When they reached their destination, Mary had never felt more ready to enjoy a day's play and pleasure.

Fresh trials awaited the little girl, however, which she had not thought of. Her bruised and bandaged cheek soon attracted the attention of her little friends. They asked many questions as to how and when she was hurt. Many times during the day Mary had to repeat her false story. Her friends sympathy, as she explained how the accident happened, tortured the little girl's mind. For she knew that many of them would have shrunk from her: they would have been enraged and astonished had they known that their little favorite Mary was a deliberate liar.

Often the poor child's cheek turned crimson with the blush of shame. Tears stood in her eyes at every fresh allusion to her wounded cheek. This anticipated day of pleasure was the most miserable the child had ever spent. Although she joined in every amusement and seemed happy like the rest, the often-repeated falsehood was a weight on her heart that she vainly tried to shake off. When they returned home in the evening, Mary pleaded fatigue as an excuse to avoid her parents' questions about the enjoyments of the day. She hurried to her little bed. When alone she gave away to her long-repressed feelings with a flood of bitter tears. She resolved to tell her mother in the morning of all her naughtiness. Comforted by this thought, Mary fell fast asleep.

Mary had made her good resolution, however, on only her own strength. As the sun dissipates the shades of night, so did all her good resolves vanish with the morning light. The tempter had again persuaded her to remain silent before she met her parents at breakfast. The tempter advised her to forget the matter altogether, if she could.

Mary found this difficult to do. Many things helped to remind her of it constantly … especially her cheek itself. In a few days, the wound healed and the bandage came off, but a scar remained on Mary's cheek. Mary's mother told her the scar would never quite fade away. This small red mark was there to remind her of the often-repeated falsehood which had scared her conscience far worse than the pitchfork had her cheek. To see the one without feeling the other was impossible. Hardly a day passed without Mary's unconfessed sin freshly entering her thoughts.

Days and weeks passed quickly away, and Charles returned again to school. Still Mary could not regain her peace of mind or silence the voice of her accusing conscience. This one unconfessed sin tarnished all her pleasures. It came between her and her God whenever she knelt to pray. It seemed a mockery to expect His love and forgiveness until she told the truth. It brought a blush of shame to her cheek whenever her parents praised or caressed her.

The child felt very sorry for her sin. She often wept and prayed to God, for Jesus Christ's sake, to forgive her. Mary tried to behave as obedient as she could. She thought this would atone for this one deception. All this brought no peace to her heart. Little Mary forgot that the proof of true repentance must be confession. As long as she shrank from this humiliation, Mary indulged the sin of pride. For she feared the loss of her parents' good opinion, not any punishment they might think necessary.

God loved this little lamb. All through these miserable weeks He would not allow Satan to harden the child's heart. He kept the little conscience active and accusing. In His own good time, He saw fit to give the necessary grace and strength to overcome that last stubborn sin of pride. God's grace and strength brought the little one humble and truly penitent to the Saviour's feet.

Chapter 3

CONFESS YOUR FAULTS ONE TO ANOTHER

"Confess your faults one to another." These words startled little Mary one Sunday afternoon at church. She looked up at the pastor with a flushing cheek and eager glance. The minister took his text from 1 John 1:8-9. "If we say that we have no sin, we deceive ourselves, and the truth is not in us. If we confess our sins, he is faithful and just to forgive us our sins, and to cleanse us from all unrighteousness." He spoke first about the obvious meaning of these verses. He told about the necessity of confession of sin before we could expect or obtain the pardon of God. This was the first part of the minister's sermon. At first little Mary listened most attentively. Then she began to wonder why, when she had so often confessed her sins to God, she could not feel at peace and forgiven by Him. It was from this thinking that the first words of this chapter had startled her. "Confess your faults one to another." They seemed like an answer to her prayers, and she listened eagerly to hear what else the preacher would say.

Before she fell asleep, her mother came into her room with the note in her hand. The child hid her face in the pillow.

The pastor explained, "Nor is the secret confession of our sins to God in all cases enough to bring peace to the wounded conscience. I am sure many of my Christian friends will agree to the truth of this. We must consider many of our sins as mainly offenses against God; for example, sins breaching the first four commandments. Many other sins are direct offenses against our neighbors as well as God. Take, for instance, the slanderer, the liar, the undutiful child, and the quarrelsome neighbor. Do not all these sin against some individual as well as sinning against God? I now address myself to such sinners. Everyone acknowledges that we cannot expect God's pardon without a full confession of our sinfulness. Many of you have experienced the peace that often follows confession to God of the sins known only to God and ourselves.

"Many of us must confess, however, the uneasiness that we still feel when remembering the unkind word or action which has wounded some loving heart. Perhaps we feel that uneasiness when we think of some slanderous tale thoughtlessly repeated, some evasion of the truth which brought blame upon another. Do we not often feel a yearning of the spirit to go and confess our faults to those we have offended? And do we not resist these kindly impulses? Are we not too proud to humble ourselves before them? We will not make the only restitution in our power. Can we then expect to feel that perfect peace which passes all understanding? We should not withhold from our friends and relatives the confession of our offenses against them, anymore than we do when we kneel in secret prayer before our God. Be sure, my friends, as long as we shrink from humbling ourselves to our fellowmen, we have pride and sin in our hearts. This sin will hinder us from receiving the nearness of Jesus Christ which is precious to the believer's soul."

Little Mary did not need to hear more. All her doubts and difficulties disappeared. She wanted the assurance of pardon through Jesus Christ. Every word of the minister's message came home to her heart. She would confess her falsehood to her dear parents; then and not until then could she feel at peace again. Little Mary lifted her heart in prayer to God. She prayed that this time He would give her strength not to waver in her good resolution.

When the service ended, Mary felt eager to get home. She wanted to set her heart at rest by the long-delayed confession. Once home she felt shy and nervous and dared not trust herself to speak to her mother. She asked for a pencil and some paper. Little Mary went to her own room and wrote this note:

Darling Mama,

I have felt very unhappy for a long time because I behaved very naughty. You remember when I hurt my cheek, we told you I fell against the corner of the big chest, but it was not so. Charles had taken a pitchfork to make our haystack bigger.

It accidentally struck my cheek. We feared to tell, for we knew he ought not to have touched the pitchfork. Now, dear Mama, you know the real truth. I have been very wicked, and I feel very sorry about that. I will pray to God to forgive me, as I hope you will. I will try with His help never to tell another lie.

Your penitent and loving child,
Mary

Little Mary then knelt down by her bed. She prayed to God, for His dear Son's sake, to forgive her sin and her long concealment of it. The little girl prayed God would help her become a better child in the future and never let her tell another falsehood. God heard the little penitent's sincere prayer. He answered it by sending down into her heart such a sweet sense of His love and forgiveness. This filled her with happiness and peace.

She left her note on her mother's dressing-table. Little Mary went downstairs to her tea with a lighter and more cheerful face than she had known for weeks.

Soon afterwards Mary went to bed. Before she fell asleep, her mother came into the room with the note in her hand. The child hid her face in the pillow. Her tears flowed fast as her mother sat down beside her and spoke kindly of the sinfulness of her past conduct. She knew her little girl realized the wickedness of lying. The mother took this opportunity, however, to again impress upon her the evils that result from lies. She told how sinful it was in God's sight and how the liar was an abomination unto Him. She went on to tell how lying destroys the happiness and confidence of a household if even one member cannot be depended on to speak the truth. "I am not sorry, my child," Mary's mother said in conclusion, "that all this has happened. You have learned by experience the misery of a guilty conscience. You have learned how little pleasure anything in this world can give us if purchased by any act of sin. You lied to avoid the possible punishment of not being able to attend a party. The party, I am sure, did not give you any pleasure to make up for the sufferings of your sensitive heart. All our love and kindness has felt like a continual reproach to you."

"Indeed it has, dear Mama," sobbed the child. "Punish me now as I deserve, and I will try to never tell another lie."

"No, my darling," replied her mother, "your papa and I think you have already suffered enough. God has punished you by all the long weeks of misery. We hope and pray that you may never forget what happened. Let it teach you, dear, never to try to conceal one fault by another. Instead we pray you have learned to bear any punishment for a first offense rather than avoid it by a falsehood. Can we trust you as we always have done as our truth-loving and truth-telling little Mary? Must we withhold our confidence from you for a time?"

"Oh, don't do that, darling Mama," cried the child as she sat up and threw her arms around her mother's neck. "It will break my heart if you won't trust me as you always have done. Indeed, indeed I won't tell another story. I have asked God to help me, and I'm sure He will. He has forgiven me now, Mama, since I wrote to you. I prayed to Him often before, but He never seemed to hear me until now. Only say you forgive me, dear Mama, and I will feel happy again.

Mary's kind mother did forgive and bless her penitent little girl. Entrusting her to the protection of Him who alone could keep her safe and give her grace to keep her good resolutions, she kissed her daughter and wished her a good night's rest.

The tears of repentance still lay wet on the child's cheeks as she fell asleep, but a smile of peace and happiness rested on her lips. Doubtless as she slept the angels of God rejoiced in heaven over the one little sinner that repented.

Mary has now grown up. On her cheek she still sees daily that small red scar, the cause of so much unhappiness, and yet, she believes, of such lasting benefit to her soul. Never while she lives will she forget the lesson she learned then or the misery of those long weeks of unconfessed sin. Mary still walks in the way that leads to everlasting life. We trust that one untruth will remain, as it has to this time, *her last* as well as her *first falsehood.*

Little readers, should any of you ever become tempted to tell an untruth, may God in His mercy make your conscience a scourge to you. May the sin lie on your conscience until it is repented and confessed. May God give you strength to keep your good resolutions. If you have fallen into this sin, may your *first* falsehood prove, like Mary's, to be your *last.*